OTHER BOOKS BY TESS MARSET:

With My Little Eye: Book One of the Mia Series

Lest We Fall: Book Two of the Mia Series

On Frogs and Princes

Like Us, The Polar Bears

The
X-Mas
Tree

by

Tess Marset

1 LONE CROW MEDIA

PUBLISHED BY

1 Lone Crow Media

www.1LoneCrowMedia.com

ISBN: 978-1-7333609-2-0

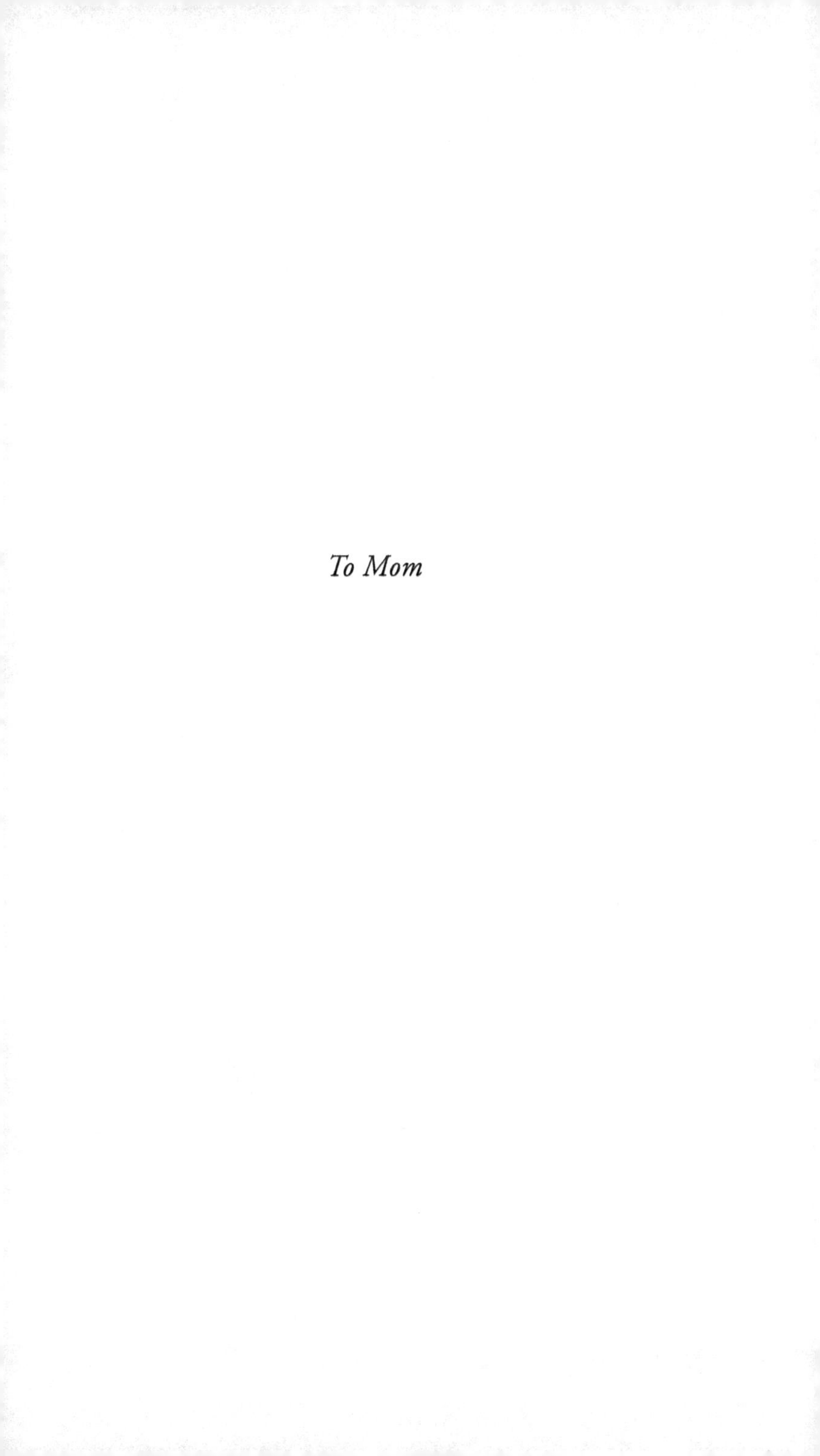

To Mom

Pop came home a little later than usual that night. We were gathered around the tube watching *Bonanza* when the door opened and we could hear his voice fill the room.

"Mama! Kids! Get your things! We are going out to celebrate." He stood in the entry with his muffler still wrapped up around his neck.

"What is it Poppa? What happened?" Ma peeked out from the kitchen as she hastily dried her hands on her apron. She came over to him, reaching up to unwrap the muffler.

"Come on Mama. Put on your coat. We can talk about it as we walk."

My sister and I tumbled over each other, running to switch off the TV and then fumbling with mittens, scarves, coats, and hats. Ma pulled off her ratty old apron and patted her hair a few times as she glanced in the entryway mirror. Pop impatiently held her heavy overcoat while she zipped up little Henry in his snowsuit that made him look like a little Eskimo. Then Nora held Henry as Ma buttoned up. Pop plopped her hat on sideways with a little pat and we were off.

We marched down the street to Chang's at a quick trot, crunching through the icy gray slush. The tiny restaurant was only five blocks away and was the celebration center of all our family good news events: graduations, anniversaries, awards, and today, a promotion. Ma quickened her pace to catch up and then started the interrogation.

"So what happened? Will you tell me already? Is it good news?" Each question reached Pop in a little cloud of frozen breath.

"I've been promoted! After ten years of wrapping needles, I've been finally moved up to the Trunk and Assembly line! It seems that Ol' Charlie retired early on account of his heart. And Mr. Kadowsky came down to the needle line and personally picked me! He said that he liked my work. It is always consistent. Of good quality. And fast too. I start tomorrow!"

Pop's face was bright. He had to carefully pick his way through the frozen slush and snowdrifts with Henry balanced on his arm, but his words flowed out in a steady excited stream.

"Wonderful, Poppa!" Ma gave his arm a squeeze through the thick sleeve. "Does this mean a raise in pay too?"

"Of course! Twenty-five dollars extra a month! What do you think - I work for nothing? You see what hard work can do for you, eh Peter?" He gave me that slow wink and nod of his head. I grinned back.

When we reached Chang's, through the steamy window we could see the waiters patiently waiting on diners seated at linen-covered tables. The smell of roast duck floated out and warmed up that cold spot on the street. We went inside.

For as long as I could remember, Pop worked for the Imperial Christmas Tree Company Incorporated. Imperial's ads boasted, 'A More Lifelike Tree, You'd Have to Cut Down.' Many times, Mom had to pick the long stiff tree needles out of Pop's work shirts before throwing them into the wash. There were a few times she missed a couple of stray needles, only to have them wind up in our socks or worse yet, our underwear.

———

Pop spent eight hours a day, six days a week winding those needles through 'twigs' that actually were only twisted wires that held the needles firmly in place. The wires were sprayed a deep forest green and tipped in brown to make them look like real pine branches. On the more expensive spruce models, tiny paper pinecones were attached here and there along the branch. Pop invented his own formula for their placement: first branch - clusters of twos and threes, five clusters total; the next branch – clusters of threes and twos, six clusters in all. "In nature, it is not always even, you know?" Pop would remind us. We could see that he took pride in his attention to detail.

And for as long as I can remember, each Christmas Pop set up our own Imperial Christmas tree. It was a Canadian Spruce Deluxe, model no. 1639. He got it the first year he started work at Imperial as a "boxer" in 1951. Over the past seventeen years, the tree has started to sag and fade a bit, but Pop refuses to get another one. He says, "This tree is built with *quality*. It is made to last for many years." Although occasionally I've seen him quietly working on it in a corner with his fine needle nose pliers, stuffing a few needles here and adding a few more cones there. One time, Nora made the mistake of saying that the tree looked like a big green bottle brush, resulting in the two of us falling out and giggling uncontrollably. Pop didn't speak to us for the rest of the evening.

On my way home from school, I passed a newly erected Christmas tree stand that stood in the vacant lot between the A&P and the Laundromat. A hand-painted sign that read 'Holiday X-Mas Trees' stretched over the entrance of the chain link fence enclosure. This was the first year a tree lot was set up there. In the past, the closest lot was at least fifteen blocks away. With our own Deluxe at home, there never was any reason to travel there.

My nostrils filled with the scent of fresh cut pine and the burning wood of a trash can fire. The tallest trees were awesome as they stretched their tops high into the cold sky. Frozen water droplets from last night's snowfall glistened on the branches. I felt compelled to stop and linger among the forest giants. I reached out to feel the needles. They glided through my grasp with surprising softness and even returned back to shape when I bent them. I let my eyes absorb the rich deep green and the rough texture of the bark.

"Hey kid, are ya buyin' or just lookin'?"

I turned around to face a squat man, cigar in mouth surrounded by three-day old stubble. His eyes were watery and sad as he studied me.

"Just looking. How much are these anyways?"

He started rattling off, pointing to various trees with his cigar now secured between his fat fingers. "You pay by the foot and the type of tree. The bigger the tree, the more you pay. The fancier the tree, the more you pay. This here is your blue spruce, fifteen bucks. That over there is your Scotch pine, ten bucks. Them trees over there are what youse call 'flocked' and they're twenty-five bucks."

"How about this one?" I pointed to a small tree standing off to the side.

"Oh, that's just your regular ol' pine, five bucks. So, are youse buyin'?" He chewed on his cigar and shoved his fists into the pockets of his hooded jacket. He obviously had grown impatient with my questions.

"Nah. I've got to ask my parents first. My pop will probably say no anyway." I took one last look at the branches soaring up to the sky.

I turned to face the man but he had already stalked away. All that was visible was his red woolen beanie cap perched above his sloop shoulders bobbing up and down through the aisles of trees. As I passed under the sign at the entrance, I noticed a tattered piece of loose-leaf paper attached to the fence with bailing wire. It read: 'Help Wanted. Part time or full time. Pack and sell trees. Good pay.'

When I got home, Henry was bawling his head off, Nora was sitting cross legged on the floor in front of the TV, and Ma was pacing the kitchen floor with my squirmy brother in her arms, stopping only to stir the steamy something in the stock pot.

"Petey, is that you?" she called past the doorway. "How was school today? Why are you so late? Listen, Poppa wants you to take down the Christmas tree from the attic today, okay? Petey?"

I nudged the side of Nora's braided head with my knee. She grunted a hello as I plopped down in the armchair and hung my leg over its arm.

"Yeah, Ma. Say Ma, what time will Pop be home tonight?"

"I'm not sure, but it will probably be late. You know it's the busy season. Why, did something happen?" she asked, always concerned that something had happened.

Pop worked a lot later these days since he got the promotion. We only saw him for a couple of hours before we went to bed. Ma tried her best to keep his dinner warm in the oven but it usually ended up dry and tough if it wasn't a soup. He typically had to put in extra hours before Christmas but this was different. Pop came home grumpy and tired. Lately, he didn't want to talk to anyone, not even her.

"No Ma, nothing happened. There's just something that I want to ask him." I said as I studied Boris Badanoff's evil grin on the screen.

"Well, wait until he's had his dinner. You know Poppa is pretty hungry when he gets home and he doesn't need a lot of questions while he's trying to eat. Make sure that you take down the tree, alright?"

Ma herself looked weary as Henry screamed and kicked his legs. She hurried up the stairs to change him.

That night, I watched as Pop unwrapped the muffler from around his neck and placed it inside his hat. He slipped out of his old coat and hung it up without a word. Ma busied herself setting out a bowl of soup, butter and bread, and a cup of coffee. She softly planted a kiss on his cheek as he sat down at the table then returned to the sink full of dishes. Nora reached out to dry another of the dripping plates in the rack while nervously glancing at Pop. After his lips mouthed a brief prayer, he silently sipped at his soup.

Earlier in the evening while helping Nora with her fraction homework, I had described to her the large live trees in the lot. Then I revealed to her the unthinkable. Nora's big brown eyes had grown even wider as she gasped, "Do you think he'll let us?"

"I don't see why not. They're not that expensive. Besides, we've never had a real tree before. Maybe just this year."

"I don't know. Poppa really likes that fake one. But I guess it's worth a try. Anything is better than that old bottlebrush. But YOU are going to have to do all the asking."

"Did I ask you to ask him? Of course I'll do all the talking. I wouldn't want to leave something this important up to you, you'll mess it up. You'll crack under the pressure."

"Oh yeah?" She stuck her tongue out and then turned back to her halves and quarters.

Now he had finished his soup. Pop wiped the last drops off his graying moustache and picked up his cup to savor his coffee. I put down the broom I was sweeping with and sat to the side of him. Fidgeting, I picked up the saltshaker shaped like a hen.

"Peter, everything going okay at school?" he asked quietly, his eyes staring ahead at the tablecloth pattern, the cup poised at his lips.

"Um uh, yeah, Pop. Everything's okay. I got a ninety percent on my algebra test today." Anything to put him in a better mood. It seemed to have worked.

"Good. Good." He went back to sipping his coffee. I felt a little more confidence building up. Nora's eyes were fixed on me. She broke for a moment only to pick up the next glass to dry, then returned her steady gaze. I knew she was waiting to see if I would be the one to crack under the pressure.

"Uh Pop, there's something I've been meaning to ask…"

"Peter, did you take down the tree today?" He looked at me now, his face haggard with exhaustion.

"Well Pop, that's what I want to ask you -"

"Didn't your mother tell you to take the tree down when you got home from school?" He spoke slowly and deliberately as he put down his cup.

"Yeah, but I wanted to –"

"What? No one listens in this house anymore? Do I have to do everything myself? All I asked was for you to do one thing for me and that was to get the tree down from the attic."

"Yeah, but Pop, I didn't bring it down because I was wondering if this year we could get a real one instead," I blurted out before I was cut off again. It was not the way I wanted things to go. Nora rolled her eyes and turned to face the dish rack. She kept her ears open, though. Henry started to fuss in his high chair. Ma continued her steady rhythm of rinsing pots but her back was rigid.

"What!" He looked at me.

"A real tree. Could we please get a real one this year? They are not that expensive. I was talking with the guy at the new tree lot on 108th and he said –"

"Am I hearing correctly? What do you want a real tree for? We've got a perfectly good tree already! Is there something you find wrong with it?" He was almost shouting.

"There's nothing wrong with it. It's just that I thought a real tree would be nice for a change."

"You thought? Well did you think about where we would get the money? You think I work hours and hours for my health? Because I like to? We don't have enough money to put clothes on your backs and food in your mouths *as it is* without you throwing away more on a useless tree that we don't even *need!*" His face was red with anger now.

Henry started to squall while Ma worked to get him out of his high chair. She wouldn't dare glance in our direction.

"But what about… what about your promotion? Don't we have extra money to –?"

"Extra money! We'll be lucky with all that *extra money* to pay our bills on time for once! If you would have done as you were told and had taken just a little bit of time to look at our tree that has served this family for years, you would see that it is better than any live tree. Just the quality and hours of hard work in it makes it look more real than a real one. You kids don't appreciate anything! You think it's easy? Just wait until you are out there breaking your back trying to support your family! The answer is NO! And don't ever ask again." Pop slammed his square fist down on the table causing the spoon and cup to jump and clatter on the saucer.

The kitchen was quiet. Nora had stopped drying a glass in mid-motion, and Ma held the baby close and stared with wide eyes. Even Henry had stopped crying and looked on with alarm. After looking at each of us to make sure his word was final, Pop then turned suddenly and left the room. Ma whirled about to give me a look that just about struck me dead in my socks. She was jiggling Henry at a furious pace in her arms.

"I, I just wanted to…" my words trailed off and my mouth fell open. I was still clutching that stupid saltshaker hen in my hand.

Nora finished her drying without saying anything to me although I could tell she didn't expect that kind of reaction from Pop.

All of a sudden we heard stomping coming down the stairs. Through the kitchen doorway we could see Pop lift the Christmas tree box off his shoulder and hurl it into the living room. It landed with a crash by the far wall. We could hear the stiff needles scratching inside their cardboard prison. The box settled crookedly on its dented corner. Pop took a deep breath through his panting, glared at us one more time, and then went upstairs where he slammed the door to his bedroom. Ma's eyes filled with tears as she shook her head and left the room.

"You really blew that one," Nora said solemnly.

"Oh, shut up."

The next morning as I pulled on my baseball jacket, I glanced over at the yellowed, water-stained tree box. It was still standing in the same position where it had landed looking like any minute it was going to topple off its crumpled corner. The faded fancy crimson and gold lettering seemed to taunt, 'Imperial Christmas Tree Incorporated. A More Lifelike Tree You'd Have to Cut Down.' I checked to see if Ma was around, then I flipped a birdie at the box as if it would have really mattered.

On the way to school, I passed by the tree lot again. I stayed on the far side of the street, not wanting to be tempted again by the bushy green trees with their strong pine scent. I spotted the red wool beanie bobbing up and down the aisles as the man stopped to haggle with a customer or pick up some windblown trash that strayed into the lot.

As I continued my pace, I could hear that nagging voice in my head that starts to get to me after a while. *Why couldn't we have a real tree for a change? Pop was just being a cheapskate. Didn't he just get a raise anyways? Anybody who is anybody gets a real tree. Did the Rockefeller Plaza put up some dumb, fake Imperial Tree? We wouldn't have to get one of those big fancy trees, even the little ones in the corner of the lot would be nice. I was – no – all of us were tired of that ugly old fake tree. Man, if I had my own money I would…*

I thought about how much money I had in my bank at home. It was a small gray bank made to look like a real safe with a red combination lock on its door. My life savings were in it – all two dollars and fourteen cents. I had forgot about buying that baseball glove in September. I considered asking Ma for the remainder of the money but she was already cutting back on everything. Come to think of it, there were a lot more cornflakes than usual in last Wednesday's meatloaf. She was saving every penny to buy Christmas presents for us. If I didn't get to the sports section or comics in time, it would be full of holes from where she had clipped coupons. In fact, I missed yesterday's Jets vs. Packers score. And she and Nora spent hours pasting green stamps in the booklets and dreaming over all of the things in the catalogue. Ma always liked to buy at least one thing that we really wanted for Christmas, sometimes even going against Pop and his Scrooge budget.

That afternoon, my mind was made up after wrestling with the decision all day. I was determined to stop in at the tree lot for one last request. Pointing to the now shredded paper tacked to the fence, I asked the man in the red wool beanie about the jobs available.

"The jobs? Yeah, I still have some positions. What? Youse interested? Have you worked with trees before?" He looked me over.

"Trees? Uh yes. I mean, no. I mean –" I didn't want to appear like I didn't know anything. "I've worked with artificial ones."

"Artificial. Huh. Can you lift? Youse don't have no bad back or nothin' do ya? Go over there and let me see you pick up that fir," he said, gesturing to a really full tree that must have been ten feet high. He watched me as he chewed on his cigar stub. I walked over to the tree and fumbled around within its boughs trying to find the trunk. Soon I had a good grasp on the rough wood and lifted with all of my strength. It was a lot heavier than the ol' Deluxe at home. A lot heavier. Still, I grunted and it raised slowly off the ground. Opening my mouth to speak, a branch jotted in, poking my tongue and nose with its needles.

The man nodded his head in approval. "Okay, okay. Put it down. Don't hurt yourself. Can you start tonight?"

I was so amazed and excited that I couldn't think clearly. Spitting out the remaining needles, I blurted, "Sure! I guess. Do I have to bring anything? Don't I have to know the names of the different trees, Mr. – uh…?"

"Name's Vito. Nah, you'll learn them as youse go along. Don't bring nothin'. You'll be helping customers with their trees – ya know – packin' 'em, tyin' 'em on their cars. The Boys will teach you how to use the Machine. Just be here at 6:30 sharp. Oh and by the way, youse get paid by the tips you earn." Vito walked off without another word, stalking a customer who had just arrived in a big Caddy.

My heart was thumping and the giddiness made me jump up to hit the big sign on my way out as I headed home. Not only was this my first job, but also I could now make some money to buy Christmas gifts and what's more, the Christmas tree. I'll show Pop yet.

Then it struck me – what was I going to tell them?

"Petey? Is that you? Why are you home so late? Is something the matter?" Ma asked as she came out of the kitchen, holding a half peeled potato in one hand and waving the peeler in the other.

"No, Ma. I was just – my friend Bob asked me if I could help him with a, uh, a *yard* job that he got. He says that he'll pay me half of what he earns." I refused to look her in the eye. She could always tell if I was lying when my eyes darted to the right. I've been working on it for the last two years since I found this out, but it is really hard to control. Tonight I did not want to take the chance of my eyes ratting me out.

"A yard job? That's good. Remember to keep up with your homework though." Just then, Henry let out a blast from his crib and Ma hurried off to put down the potato and fetch him.

"A yard job? In the snow? What kind of job is that?" Nora wriggled a suspicious nose at me. I couldn't decide if she would make a better lawyer or private eye.

There was no use in trying to get around her, as she was an avid snoop, so I fessed up. "Okay, it's not a yard job. I got a job in the big Christmas tree lot around the block. I start tonight. But don't you breathe a word of this to Ma or Pop."

"How much do you get paid?" Nora's eyes narrowed.

"Just tips… Wait a minute. Oh no, I'm not paying you anything."

Her eyes stayed narrowed and one of her eyebrows arched.

"Look, if you keep your big mouth shut, I promise I'll buy you a nice Christmas present this year."

"No more socks for my doll?"

"No. Something nicer, okay?" I gave her my most sincere face. Nora melted.

"Okay. Besides, I know you are doing this so you can get us a real tree, right?"

She was amazing.

"Right. So cover for me. I've got to do my homework now. I start at 6:30."

I was able to slip out of the house before Pop came home, leaving Ma and Nora to fill him in on the details of my 'yard job.' I could trust Nora to come up with a good enough reason for me to work on a yard after dark. I just had to make sure I remembered to ask her later what it was. Outside it was already night and the temperature was dropping rapidly but the string of bulbs that surrounded the lot made it look bright and exciting as I approached.

I worked until ten o'clock straight, toting trees for customers, hoisting them upon car top after car top, stopping briefly to thaw myself by the trashcan fire with the rest of the gang. It turned out the Machine was just a galvanized trashcan with the bottom cut out. I learned quickly to feed the tree top-first through the hole. This held the branches together for me to bind them tightly with the twine Vito cheaply doled out in short lengths. For the entire evening, I had only talked with him long enough to be pointed in the right direction when I first entered the lot. After that, I rarely saw him unless a customer in an expensive vehicle pulled up.

The rest of the gang was more talkative when we could spare a few minutes between hauling and twining. The guys mostly ranged in ages close to my own fifteen years and older. We shot the bull about where we went to school and what we were going to do with all of our earnings, all the while holding out our hands to catch the heat off the burning cut tree branches and stubs in the can. The smoke from the fire stung our eyes causing us to constantly wipe at them with our smudgy fingers. As for pay, the customers for the most part were pretty generous. One of the Eng brothers told me that the tips would get even better as Christmas approached.

That night, before the makeshift chain link gate at the lot was closed and padlocked, I counted out the money I had worked so hard for. Tonight, my first night on the job, I had made $7.75. Exhaustion and sore muscles couldn't crowd out the little shiver of success I felt as I shoved the money back into my jacket pocket. I withdrew my hand to find one of the quarters sticking to it from tree sap.

After I had been working for a couple of weeks, one afternoon, I was surprised to hear Pop's voice in the kitchen when I came home from school. He spoke to Ma in low tones but I could make out a few phrases like "pushing the line too hard" and "that sonnabitch Kadowsky." Nora glanced up from her daily viewing of *Bullwinkle* when I entered. She lay on the floor with her elbows propped up and her head cupped in her hands. Henry sat close by in his playpen chewing on a wooden spoon.

I came around to the front of her and silently mouthed, "What's going on?"

She didn't bother to play along. In a plain voice she answered, "Pop came home early today 'cause he hurt his hand." Her eyes never left the screen.

"Is he okay?"

"Yeah. Ma's just rebandaging it. From what I could hear, he cut it on a jagged piece of wire. He says it's because Mr. Kadowsky is rushing everyone so much to put out lots of trees, that he won't let them take the time to finish the wires right. He sounds pretty mad."

Heeding her warning, I approached the kitchen with caution. Ma and Pop were engrossed in the bandaging as Pop held out his hand and Ma wrapped the white gauze around and around. A red stain appeared immediately on the fresh bandage as the blood continued to seep through. They didn't notice me as I poured a glass of milk and grabbed a few cookies until I sat down across the table from them.

"Hi Petey. I didn't hear you come in. How was school today?" Ma managed a small worried smile as she turned away from her work momentarily to greet me. Pop, too, looked at me. He had dark circles under his eyes and his face looked worn. It had been days since I had seen him last.

"It was okay. How're you feeling, Pop?"

"This? This is nothing. Just a little scratch. Nothing for you to worry about. How's your yard job coming along?" He winced a little as Ma tied the knot.

"My yard job?" I almost forgot about that. "Oh fine. Yeah, it's going great. Tony knows a lot of people who need their sidewalks shoveled and their branches cut back."

"Tony? What happened to your friend, Bob?" Ma asked me. I guess she was listening that day.

"Uh, I work with both Bob *and* Tony now. Tony knew more places and he wanted in, so we split everything three ways now." I shoved a cookie in my mouth and concentrated on making my eyes look straight ahead.

"That reminds me of a job I had when I was a boy," Pop interjected. "Ernst and I shoveled so much so snow! You are doing a good job for those people, Peter?"

I nodded and kept chewing.

"Good. Good. You do the job right, then they want you to return for perhaps another job. That's exactly what I keep trying to tell that sonna-" Ma shot him a look. He received it and continued, "- that *knucklehead* Kadowsky. People don't want to buy junk. I try to tell him but do you think he would listen? Enough! I am tired of talking about that place." When Pop buttoned up, a stillness settled over the kitchen.

Later, we had dinner like we use to what seemed like long ago, with Ma and Pop gabbing about who was doing what in the neighborhood and all of us sharing a few jokes and bits of news. Nora recited the first five stanzas of *Hiawatha* that she had learned at school, only messing up once. Every time she said, "Gitchee-gumee," Henry would repeat "Gumee" and clap his hands. We all cracked up. Then it was time for me to return to the tree lot while Pop stayed home with the rest of our family in our small living room. It was strange to see him kick back in his easy chair. He looked so relaxed and peaceful for once. I suddenly wanted to hang up my jacket and plop down on the floor between everyone but I knew Vito would chew me out if I missed a day.

Strangely feeling homesick, I slowly slipped my arms into my sleeves. Tonight was going to be a busy one at the lot with it being Friday. I knew I would be dead tired and sore when I got home. When I was all zipped up, I stopped at the doorway to say goodbye. I was kind of hoping they would see my face, ask me what was wrong, and tell me to stay home. Instead they all waved goodbye without leaving their seats and returned to watching *Creature Feature* on the tube.

In the entryway, I could hear Pop saying his usual when I opened the door – "Oh now, how could that happen? What is with these people? Can't they see that the monster is just around the corner?" Then Nora would giggle, "Oh Pop, it's only a movie." It was a small game they liked to play. The door shut out the warmth and voices behind me as I stepped out onto the stoop that led down to the street. I reluctantly went down the stairs, turned and crunched my way up the darkened avenue, alone.

Suddenly, it was the day before Christmas. Being on winter break, I had no school but it meant I had to come in early with the rest of the guys to handle the all day crush of customers. Trees were selling out fast. Between waves of selling, twining, and hauling, I went to choose the tree I would take home tonight. I now looked over the trees with an expert eye, immediately noticing any small flaws and imperfections. I could judge which tree was fresh by running my hands through the needles and inhaling its scent. I thought back to the first day I had wandered into the lot weeks ago when I was awed by the trees' towering size and aliveness, and I had to laugh.

I decided to go for a seven-foot blue spruce, the most expensive of the unflocked trees. I swiftly set the tree on the sawhorse and sawed the bottom inch or so off the trunk. Slipping it in to the Machine, the tree was bound. Whipping out the hammer, I nailed an 'X' made of pine slats to the bottom to make a stand. The tree was then placed in a dark corner well out of the way of desperate customers looking at the last minute for the perfect tree. To be on the safe side, I scribbled a note with a piece of charred wood on a scrap of paper and stuck it to the tree: SOLD. I took out the small wad of bills in my pocket, thumbed out fifteen bucks and handed them to Vito. Feeling good, I even drew out an extra dollar to give him as a tip. He grunted as he took the money without a second glance at me. He counted it, his fingers moving quickly in his fingerless gloves, then shoved it all into his jeans pocket and walked away.

Just as Dennis Eng had said, the tips did increase as Christmas approached. I had kept the growing pile of cash stowed carefully in my tiny wall safe at home. Then this past weekend, I walked down to the Boulevard to shop for the family. I was able to find a pretty crystal bowl for Ma as well as a new robe. For Pop, I picked out a hand carved pipe made from mahogany, a small great smelling sack of tobacco, and a pair of warm leather gloves. Keeping my promise to Nora, I quickly skipped over the fifty cent doll socks and went straight for a tall walking doll with long brown braids like her own and a couple of doll outfits. I even found a stuffed bunny and a small wooden train for Henry. After that, I had enough left over to buy the portable transistor radio that I had always wanted – the one small enough to fit in my pocket with an earplug cord that reached all the way up to my ear. I felt like a king spending the profit that I had made from hauling trees. I felt even richer knowing that I still had another fifty-seven dollars stowed away in my safe.

That evening when the trees sold out, the gang and I were anxious to get home. As we slipped out of the lot, we gathered for a moment to wish each other a Merry Christmas then scattered in all directions. I walked past the darkened A&P proudly hoisting the spruce up on my shoulder. I thought *Just wait 'til Pop gets a load of this. And he can't say anything about the money either. I did this all myself without any of his help.*

When I entered the house, I was greeted by a squeal from Nora.

"Oohhh! You got it! I knew you would! Oohh, Mama! Come look! See what Pete brought home!" She danced all about me as I looked for a place to set it down. "Hurry up! Cut the cords!" she insisted.

I wound up setting it down in the only space I could find, next to the Deluxe tree already decked out in our ancient decorations and garland. Ma must've decorated it with Nora sometime. I knew Nora didn't do it alone because she tends to bunch all the decorations in clumps and the icicles hang on just the forward side of the tree.

"What is going on out here? Nora, what is the–" Ma entered the living room looking for my sister then stopped in her tracks when she saw the towering tree. "Oh my God!" she said, placing her hand by her mouth and gazing up at the tree in amazement.

"Surprise!" Nora yelled, immediately taking possession of the tree. I laughed and held Henry up to touch the branches.

"How did you…? Where did you…?" Ma was at a loss for words yet there was a look of pleasure and wonderment that filled her face. Then suddenly she asked, "Peter, you didn't cut down someone's tree, did you?" She turned a hard gaze at me.

"What? Oh no Ma. No. I swear! I got the money to buy it from my yard job."

"Oh, well, it's beautiful. Just lovely." Ma, too, was stroking the soft needles while taking in the sight and scent of the tree. "So green! It didn't cost you a lot?"

"No, not too much. Besides it is worth it just to see your faces when I brought it in," I said softly as I looked at Ma and then the tree. Through the corner of my eye, I caught her bright smile. I could feel my chest fill with the pride of knowing that I had done this all myself. I could feel my childish days of receiving had just ended now knowing what it was to provide.

We all stared at the tree for a few moments more, touching and admiring its aliveness. Being shook from her dreamlike state, Ma struck upon a realization.

"Speaking of faces, what is your Poppa going to say when he sees this?" she asked with apprehension.

"Mama, you won't let him take it away, will you?" Nora whined.

My chest deflated. "I – I don't care what he says." I felt a twinge of queasiness enter my gut.

Ma's eyes grew large as she came around to face me. "What was that you said?"

The queasiness continued to rumble around in there until it was kicked out by a cold hard defiance.

"I said I don't care what he says," I repeated but this time I felt totally justified in saying it. "All he was worried about was the money. Well, I worked my butt off for this tree so he shouldn't have anything to say about it."

"Peter! How could you say such a thing! And watch your mouth."

"No Ma, you know it's true. We all wanted a real tree, except for him. But he was being pigheaded and cheap about it. He didn't care at all about what we wanted. What does he think? That that old broken down bottlebrush of a tree is going to last forever? All I needed was five lousy bucks. Heck, I made that my first night of work."

The smirk on my face was erased by a stinging slap. Ma looked at the angry red print she left on my cheek then her own hand in wonder. Nora stared in amazement at the scene but then her own face flushed red and she turned away in embarrassment for me.

Swallowing hard to choke down the knot forming in my throat, my eyes welled up with tears but I was determined not to cry. As I stood there with my mouth gaping open, I looked at my mother's face as if for the first time. Seeing this, Ma's own eyes became moist but she straightened her back to stand very erect.

"It is not just the money. You don't understand all that he does for you, all that he wants for you – dreams for you. Someday you will know." She stopped but then added, "He is your *father*, Peter." With this, she left the room. I could hear her crying and sniffling in the kitchen as she returned to the chore of preparing our dinner.

The slap across my face could have been replaced with a kick to my stomach as I watched Ma walk away. I looked back at the mighty spruce, but all of its magic seemed to have melted away. It could have been any one of the hundred trees we had at the lot. Even Nora felt a little ashamed to look at it now. She chose to focus her attention on settling Henry back into his playpen.

We waited for Pop to come home to join us for our Christmas Eve dinner. It was a quiet somber wait mixed with anticipation and growing anxiety. Neither Ma nor I spoke except for small obvious statements. We waltzed stiffly around each other never letting our eyes meet. I felt tempted to throw the tree into the backyard but as I looked at it, I couldn't help but feel some sort of protectiveness towards it.

Just then, the front door opened and Pop stepped in. His shoulders sagged and his feet barely seemed to clear the floor. Sensing that all of our eyes were upon him, he looked at each of our faces, seeing us but not seeing us at the same time. At that moment, he looked so old that it was hard to believe that it was the same old Pop.

Then he saw the tree.

Without a word, he turned and headed back out the door. I was all prepared to explain, all set to tell him everything – the tree, the lot, my earnings. Now he was gone.

Ma looked at me in consternation. "Peter, get on your coat and go after him. You thought you were man enough to defy your father, now be man enough to apologize to him."

I grabbed my baseball jacket in my hand and was out the door. As I walked I wriggled it on to escape the chill biting at me. I thought I saw him heading down the street to the subway through the falling snow.

"Pop! Pop! Wait up!" I called after him, but he kept walking.

Slipping through the dirty snow that was now turning to ice, I finally caught up with him and grabbed him by his shoulder. The very frightened face of a man suspecting he was about to be mugged greeted me instead.

"Uh, sorry. I was looking for my father," I said but he didn't look convinced.

Craning my neck in the other direction, I could make out a more familiar stride down the block and just clearing the corner candy store. As I rounded the corner, I could see the darkened A&P down the street. There was not a soul on either of the sidewalks from what I could make out in the yellowish circles of light cast by the street-lights. It seemed that everybody was home enjoying their holiday meals. I was about to turn back when I spotted him.

Pop was this lone solitary figure sitting there on a bus bench. I crossed the frozen street but he didn't even look up at me. I recognized my now-empty tree lot across the street as I approached and sat down. Still, he said not a word. We sat for a few minutes in silence, each of us taking turns looking at the darkened lot. I was trying to feel out his anger but surprisingly, I couldn't detect any. Instead there seemed to be a sense of sadness about him.

"Pop, about the tree. You see, I – I was just trying to surprise everyone. I bought it with my own money, so you wouldn't have to."

There was no response. He stared straight ahead.

"I wasn't trying to make you angry or anything. I mean, the Imperial Deluxe is good – great in fact, but we just wanted something different this year. S-so I got a job at that tree lot to pay for a real tree. And I thought, just maybe this year, if it was free and all, you wouldn't mind."

Still he said nothing. He directed his gaze down at his hand that had been rewrapped once again this morning, the gauze tattered and gray from a day's work.

"I wasn't trying to hurt your feelings or nothing." Suddenly that hard lump formed in my throat again.

We sat in the cold circle of light on that silent street for I don't know how long. Pop didn't stir. He kept his eyes down. My hands jammed deep into my pockets, I started to shiver and my leg started to jog up and down. Why wouldn't he say something? How long was he going to sit there? I was beginning to get really worried.

Finally, a very quiet voice, a very tired voice seeped out of Pop.

"You think this is about a tree?" His eyes now fixed on the lot across the street.

"Well, um, yeah. I mean, isn't it?" I was confused.

"You think this is about a tree!" he repeated, his voice climbing in the still air. Then Pop's shoulders started to shake. He covered his face with his hands and rubbed hard.

I suddenly felt scared and horrible and guilty all at once.

"Pop? Ah come on, Pop. I'm sorry. I really am. I didn't mean to hurt you or Ma or anybody." I reached over and clung to the shaking man. "I'm – I am sorry Poppa."

He opened his arms and engulfed me in a hug, my tears soaking into his winter coat. His hug grew fierce until he was actually squeezing the air out of me. Then with my head cradled against his broad chest, I could start to make out sounds not of sobbing, but his low rumble of a laugh. It was a silent laugh concealed under spasms and winter clothing but soon it erupted to the surface and spilled and tumbled out from underneath his moustache.

I didn't know at all what to expect next, so I waited for him to get a hold of himself and stop laughing. He was still holding me in his arms when he threw back his head and took a deep breath. Then he released me and letting out a big sigh, he looked at me as if I was as small as Henry.

Pop said, chuckling tenderly, "Peter. You have never hurt me. What? Getting a tree hurt your Poppa? There is no tree in the world that could do that. No Peter, it is much more than that. Much more." He grew quiet. "Today I lost my job."

"What!" My ears had to be lying.

"My job. At Imperial Christmas Tree Company Incorporated. I lost it. After seventeen years of hard work and dedication. Would you believe it?" The laughter was all played out now leaving Poppa tired and gray.

"No Pop, no. What happened? Was it Mr. Kadowsky?"

"It was Kadowsky, then again, it wasn't Kadowsky. It was something else Peter. Something very hard to understand. *I* don't even understand it. All I know is that all they want is faster, faster, faster. Everything must go faster. They said 'The line must be speeded up. We must have higher production.' But they pay no attention to how the trees turn out. And I say to them, 'No, that isn't right. A customer pays for this tree, I am going to give them a good tree.' It may be artificial. It may be fake. Hell, it may even look like a bottlebrush…"

Thank goodness Pop wasn't looking at me when he said this or he would have noticed the shame burning through my cheeks.

He continued, "…but not only do I give them a tree, I give them the *best* tree that I can make."

"They didn't want that?" I felt so naïve.

"When I first started working at Imperial, maybe they wanted the best. Then they want not only the best but they wanted *more*. After a while in order to work so quickly, they didn't care about doing the best anymore and quality and pride and doing the job right was forgotten. But you know Peter, I won't forget about doing my best. I can't. Forgetting that will not only cheat the customer, it would cheat *me*. And it would cheat you and Mama and Nora and Henry. *That* I couldn't do. You understand this?" he asked me. Although my mind at the moment was a jumble, I nodded.

"So I said, 'To hell with you Kadowsky! To hell with Imperial Tree Company!' And he said, 'What was that you said?' And I said, 'You heard me you sonnabitch!' So he said, 'Get out! Get out! You're fired!' So I got out. And here I am. Actually, there was more but… Enough! I am tired of talking about that place."

"But Pop, what will you do? What will happen to all of us?"

"I'm not sure what will happen to us. You see, some-times you say things that seem like the right idea at the time but then when you think about it later, you wish you could undo what you've said. Yes, I said that to Kad-owsky but what was I going to tell you children and your Mama? Then when I saw all your faces waiting for me, I – I couldn't find the words to explain what had happened," Pop said, his voice breaking before his words trailed off.

He returned to sitting very quietly again, the snow falling and piling up on his shoulders. He reminded me of the old forgotten statue of General Pershing that was in the corner of the park by the overpass. I suddenly felt the urge to take him in my arms to shelter him from the snow that continued to fall. When I started to reach for him, I noticed that his eyes were wet. A sense of alarm washed over me again and instead I grabbed a hold of his hand. It's funny how his hand didn't feel as large as it did when we used to walk up and down the beach when I was a kid. Feeling my hand on his, he hastily wiped at his eyes and turned his face away.

"You'd think, after seventeen years of work. Seven-teen years of my life…"

We sat for a while again. Looking at the tree lot across the street, my mind was flooded with the very recent memories of working there. A cold realization sank in – could I do such a job for seventeen years? Would I last? Could I even survive one year there? Now that it was Christmas, I was glad that I wouldn't have to return. Getting paid felt good and buying things with my own money felt even better. But I thought about Pop and the millions of times he walked out that door to work. Even when he was sick or when he hadn't gotten any sleep, like the time he stayed up all night to fix the broken pipe in the basement. I never gave much thought to what he was doing at work all day – until now. Each day going back to the same chore of twisting wires and dealing with bosses; for longer than I had been alive.

Although he put in many days and many hours, at the end of each month he and Ma still had to decide which bill would have to wait or where else they could cut corners. Yet Nora and Henry and I always seemed to have what we needed and sometimes we even got things we wanted. What if *I* had a family who looked to me to provide? What would I say to them if I lost my job? I felt I needed to make it up to Pop somehow. I had lied to this man who had done for me all my life without ever a complaint.

"Pop?"

He didn't answer but continued to sort and turn things over in his head.

"Poppa?"

"Yes, Peter."

"I have a little money saved up from my job. It's not a whole lot but I want you to have it."

"No, you keep your money. You've worked hard to earn it. There are so many things a boy wants that I cannot get. You keep your money and spend it on something you want."

"But Pop, this is something I want. Please, say you'll take it when we get home," I pleaded with him, searching out the answer in his grey eyes.

Sensing my urgency, he allowed himself to consider it for a few moments. Then he simply replied, "No."

Pop suddenly smacked my knee then clutched it. His old energy slowly started to flow once more.

"Not to worry Peter. You will get old like me very soon if you worry so much. I may have lost my job but Imperial Tree Company Incorporated lost their most valuable employee today. And money? Of course we need it, but I think that we'll survive. The most important thing is that we are all together. We have our health. And although I may throw a tree box or two, I think we are happy, no?" He took another deep breath and then continued, "Maybe the day after Christmas I'll call your Uncle Freddie. They're always looking for valuable employees like me to work at the shoe factory."

"But you hate the shoe factory! And Uncle Freddie said–"

"Pah! Uncle Freddie! I need a job. I will get a job. And I will make the best damned shoes that I can while I am there *when* I get the job." His mouth was set in determination.

It all started to come together in my head: what Ma had said and the trees and Pop, and although I couldn't collect my thoughts long enough to have it make sense yet, I knew that someday soon, it would.

"Besides that, you're rich now, eh? Maybe I should take a looonnngg vacation instead and let you work for a while- Hey! What is this red mark on your face now?" He grasped my face in his hand and turned my slapped cheek toward the light.

Summoning up my best impression of him, I answered, "This? This is nothing. Just a little red mark. Nothing for you to worry about."

My voice still wasn't as deep as his but I know I got the accent right. He chuckled as he recognized himself. Then his eyes flashed with pride as he looked me over and tousled the snowflakes out of my hair.

"You're getting cold Petey. How's about we head home now. Mama cook anything good for our dinner tonight?"

We lifted ourselves stiffly from the bench and turned to make our way back to the house. The quietness of the snowfall about us muffled out the great noise of the surrounding city. All that was left was the crunching of our footsteps in the frozen snow as we walked side by side down the dark street.

"Oh Peter, by the way, you don't tell Mama what I said."

"What? About losing your job?" I felt that I was now being included in a man's confidence. I grew very sober with the seriousness of it.

"That we tell her later. We won't ruin her Christmas; she works so hard for it to be just right. Nah. About the 'hells' and 'sonnabitch,' okay?" He gave me that slow wink as the twinkle in his eye returned.

We reached the warm welcome of home and family as we entered through the front door. Mama for once, did not greet us with her usual 'What's the matter?' A searching glance at Pop's face told her what she needed to know at that moment. After we hung our jacket and coat, Ma and Nora continued to huddle about us, following us into the living room. Then Pop looked up at the spruce. He studied it carefully from its tallest point down to the X of slats nailed to the bottom.

Finally, he said, "Yes Peter. It is a fine tree. You selected well."

I was surprised that everyone couldn't hear my sigh of relief. What he did next was even more surprising. He went over to where the Imperial Deluxe was standing in its traditional corner and reaching high up amongst the wire branches, he took the star off its top. Turning towards the spruce, Pop stretched up his arm and standing even taller on his tiptoes, he grabbed near the top, bent the branch over, and placed the star on it.

"There. I knew something was missing." He looked at Nora and me and scolded, "Come on! Aren't you going to finish decorating?"

We hesitantly approached the Imperial Deluxe with its faded drooping branches. Before we reached for any of the ornaments, we stopped and turned to Pop in one last question of approval.

"Go on. Go on. We need to decorate this tree. It's so big! I don't know if we'll have enough to fill it."

After his permission was granted, we grew more and more enthusiastic about transferring the timeless decorations from the fake tree to the live one. At that rate, the Imperial Deluxe was quickly and thoroughly relieved of any and all that had decorated it. It sat stripped and faded in the corner; a few of its crumbling paper pinecones had fallen off and rolled around the base. The spruce stood gloriously alive and overshadowing, its fresh branches holding up the glass decorations to the light.

During our redecorating, Pop had slipped quietly from the room only to return with the dilapidated dented tree box. And just as quickly as we had decorated the spruce, Pop dismantled the Imperial Deluxe, expert hands folding the branches to fit neatly within. From there, he hoisted the tree box up on his shoulder and walked instead to the kitchen, not up to the attic.

Ma opened her mouth to protest, "Poppa! What are you doing? Where are you going-" She stopped once she realized his intentions.

"Peter! Come! Open the door for your Poppa!" Pop's voice carried throughout the house.

We went down the few steps from the landing to the back door. There, I held open the door and screen for him. I watched as he let the tree box drop down carelessly on its side in front of the row of trashcans that stood against the house. Its slogan, 'A More Lifelike Tree You'd Have to Cut Down' read upside down in a helpless position. We watched as the rapid snowfall stuck to the box and soon covered the lettering until it was no longer visible.

"But Pop, there was nothing wrong with that tree. Why did you get rid of it? I thought we'd keep it and could take it back out next year or something." It felt like a childhood memory had been left out in the darkness and snow.

"There are some things that we just can't keep holding onto, Peter. Come, let's go inside and have some dinner."

With that, he closed the door to the cold and we returned to the warmth.